My Allah Series
Allah Listens to Everyone

Kisa Kids Publications

Parents' Corner

إِنَّ رَبِّي لَسَمِيعُ الدُّعَاءِ

Surely, my Lord hears Duʿāʾ
(Sūrat Ibrāhīm, Verse 39)

Dear Parents/Guardians,

One of the reasons older children may struggle with prayer is because they do not truly understand the blessings of this gift. Therefore, it is vital for parents to instill this understanding in their children at an early age to help them develop their love for communicating with Allāh.

Remind children that Allāh, the Most Merciful, has created them and takes care of them. He has given us the beautiful gift of being able to talk to Him wherever we are and whenever we want! A good way to instill this love of communicating with Allāh is by showing them how you, as parents, give priority to salāh and duʿa. When they see their parents yearning to talk to Allāh, inshāAllāh they will be even more eager than you! In addition, providing your children with a nice salāh kit (including an attractive sajjadah, perfume, tasbiḥ, and special prayer clothes) can also instill love and excitement for prayer.

This book encourages children to create a spiritual connection with the Almighty by introducing them to the concept and practice of duʿa or supplication. InshāAllāh, this book will help strengthen the love your children already have for Allāh and instill the desire to communicate with Him at all times.

With Du'as,
Kisa Kids Publications

Let's begin with Bismillah, and look around, far and near.
Let's travel the world to see what languages we can hear!

In what language(s) do you speak to Allah?

On a farm in India, a man stands next to his scarecrow.
He prays in Hindi, "O Allah, please help my plants and crops grow!"

What kind of help do you need from Allah?

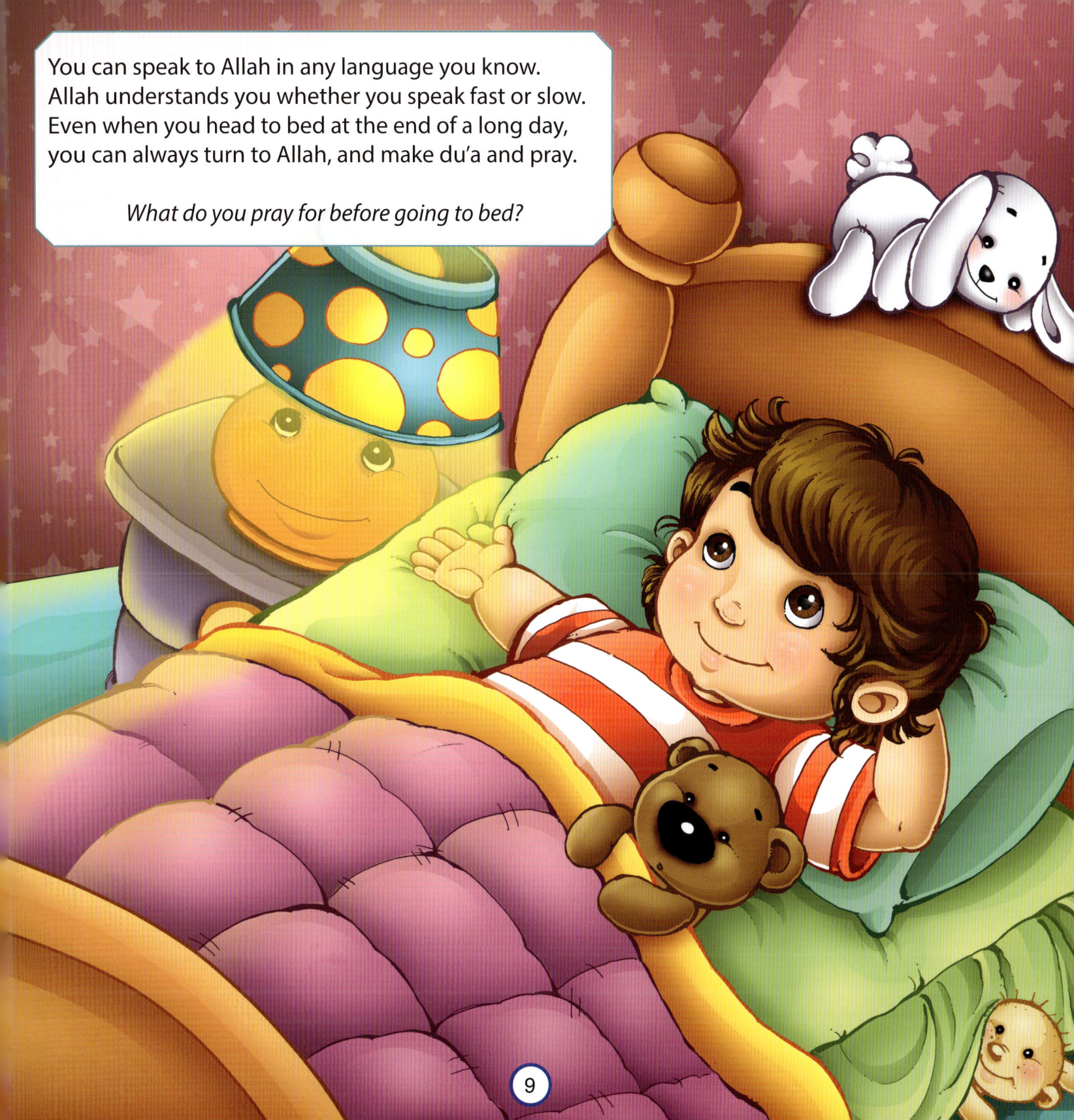

You can speak to Allah in any language you know. Allah understands you whether you speak fast or slow. Even when you head to bed at the end of a long day, you can always turn to Allah, and make du'a and pray.

What do you pray for before going to bed?

If you sit quietly on a swing,
Allah will still know exactly what you think.

So, you see, Allah is always listening carefully,
to your prayers and mine.
So go ahead, talk to Him in any language, at any place, and at any time!

What will you say to Allah today?